three shots

KATY GRANT

An imprint of Enslow Publishing
WEST 44 BOOKS™

Please visit our website, www.west44books.com.
For a free color catalog of all our high-quality books, call toll free 1-800-398-2504.

Cataloging-in-Publication Data
Names: Grant, Katy.
Title: Three shots / Katy Grant.
Description: New York : West 44, 2023. | Series: West 44 YA verse
Identifiers: ISBN 9781978596535 (pbk.) | ISBN 9781978596528 (library bound) | ISBN 9781978596542 (ebook)
Subjects: LCSH: Children's poetry, American. | Children's poetry, English. | English poetry.
Classification: LCC PS586.3 G736 2023 | DDC 811'.60809282--dc23

First Edition

Published in 2023 by
Enslow Publishing LLC
2544 Clinton Street
Buffalo, NY 14224

Editor: Caitie McAneney
Designer: Katelyn E. Reynolds

Photo Credits: Cvr Shane White/Shutterstock.com, cvr (texture) donatas1205/Shutterstock.com

Printed in the United States of America

CPSIA compliance information: Batch #CW23W44: For further information contact Enslow Publishing LLC at 1-800-398-2504.

Three Shots

rang out
during the night
while I slept not
knowing.

One-two.
Three.

Those three shots
ended three lives.
Broke many hearts.
Hurt more people
than I can count.

Shattered
my
world
forever.

Three Days Before

Everything was normal.
I thought.

Friday after school,
I text my friend Gracie,
Down for a street sesh?

YES! Always, she answers.

So I grab my board and
head to our meet-up spot.
Halfway between our houses.
First week in November.
Perfect weather.
Sunny, 80 degrees.
Not too hot.
The long
long
long desert summer
finally over.

Gracie comes pushing down the street.
Nollies over a dead palm frond.
"Dope!" I yell.

She looks up, laughs.
"Le's getit!"
She's slim, athletic.
Sun-streaked hair
falls out of a ponytail.
T-shirt sleeves rolled up
like always.

The thing about skating street is
just the fun of looking for
all that's skateable.
Finding the challenge.
Being creative.

Nothing like spotting an obstacle
a little too high, kinda awkward.
Maybe has a lousy run-up.
Scoping how you'll hit it.

Skating only parks you get lazy.
Every ledge, rail, box waxed buttery.
So on days like today, you go
prowl for some new spots
you're gonna want to skate
forever.

Street Sesh on a Friday

We're flowing the streets.
Landing flatground tricks.
Heel flips, pop shuv-its,
the *whir whir whir* of
wheels skimming hot asphalt.

Gracie's always progressing.
Today it's a
no-comply 180 nosegrab.
"First try?" I say.
"First try!" she says.

She then misses it
five, six, seven …
"You're this close," I say.
"I gotta commit," she says.

She keeps at it—
lands on the bolts.
"That had steez," I say.
"I'll take it," she says,
a sly smile spreading
across her face.

I land a bs 360
on flat first try.
Gracie rates it,
"Sicker than sickkk!"

We skate to a church parking lot,
empty on a Friday.
Doing slappy crooks on curbs,
ollying down a three-stair.

Doing a 50-50 on
this ledge. It's tough the way
it curves in, curves out.
Then a sharp curve
spits you out real quick.
Have to get just
the right speed.

Gracie's boardsliding
the parking blocks.
I'm waxing the handrail
down the ramp
'bout to hit it
when a door opens.
Lady peeks out at us.

We say hi, tell her
we're just leaving.
Thank her for
the use of the lot.
Skate away laughing.

Perfect vibe of another
sweet street sesh.

Dinner—Not

We skate to Gracie's house.
Go inside for some gaming.
Munch on kale chips, hummus,
and water.
(Her mom's idea of snack food.)

We kill zombies and race go-karts.
Gracie shows me her latest painting,
Watermelon: Expiration Date.
Her abstract art comes into focus
as soon as I hear the title.

She tells me about cutting open
a watermelon, dropping some of it
on the floor, splattering jagged
green and red chunks.

Other canvases, some half-finished,
lean in stacks against her walls.
Faint smell of linseed oil always
hanging in the air of her room.

Her little brother comes in.
Stands in the doorway.

Abe is

quiet.
A nice kid.
Skinny, blond, preppy.
Geography whiz.
Plays alto sax in his
junior high band.
("Second chair!" Gracie always says—
whatever that means.)
I guess he's pretty good.

When Gracie and I hang out,
Abe is usually around,
politely waiting
to be invited.

Gracie's mom, Mindy,
calls out from the other room,
"Can you make dinner for
you and your brother?"

Gracie says, "Sure."
Nudges me with her elbow.
"You know Daniel's here, right?
He's staying for dinner."

A long pause and then
Mindy asks Gracie to
come talk to her.
Voices mumbling mumbling.

I picture Mindy's
serious expression.
Looking tired,
slightly stressed.

Gracie comes back, rolls her eyes.
"Sorry, she says she wants
a *quiet* evening.
Just the three of us."

A shy smile spreads over
Abe's face. He says,
"No loud Daniels allowed."
We all laugh at that.

We talk about weird mom
rules. Like—no phones
at the dinner table, use a
coaster for that glass.

I tell Gracie no worries,
I'm spending the weekend
with my dad and his girlfriend.
Gracie asks how the baby talk
is going. I say, it's not.
(Carrie wants one, Dad doesn't.)

So I grab my board, fist bump Abe.
Tell Gracie I'll see her Monday.
"See ya, Dez!" Gracie says.
Short for my last name—Valdez.
(Only Gracie calls me that.)

I skate home happy.
The whole weekend
lies ahead of me.
No worries.

The First Sign

that something might be wrong
is the unanswered texts.

Sunday night at 10:30, I text Gracie,
Can you figure out the chemistry homework?
I don't get why there's so much math in … science.
(Angry emoji face.)

No answer.
911!
If I flunk the test Friday
it's on you.
(Winking emoji face.)

Still no answer.
Which I guess means
she's asleep.

So I text Trevor.
He's got my back,
talks me through it.

I don't even think about
the unanswered texts.

Where Are You??

Monday morning Gracie is not
in the courtyard.
Her best friend Lydia
is looking for her, too.

"I've texted like five times," says Lydia.
"She's not answering."

"Maybe she's sick," I say.

"Too sick to answer a
freaking text?"

I shrug. Pull out my phone.
Hey where are you??
You're LATE! I text.

Still no answer.

The Announcement

I'm in English. First Hour.

Ten minutes before the bell,
a student messenger knocks.
Comes inside, hands Mr. Chamberlain
a message.

I see his face change
as he reads it.
We all feel it.

A long pause.

Mr. Chamberlain clears his throat.
"I have some ... terrible news."

Is his hand shaking?

"I'm really sorry to tell you this."

His voice so soft we all lean
forward.

"Gracie Sullivan, her brother Abe,
who's a seventh grader at Hayden,
and their mother
have all
passed away."

A gasp.

"*WHAT?*" yells Anthony Yazzie.
Lashonda Wilkes starts sobbing.

"Grief counselors will be
made available immediately."

More noise and talk.

Everyone grabs their phones.

But all I hear is
my own heartbeat in my ears.

Pounding. Pounding. Pounding.

Here But Not Here

In the halls,
past classrooms.
A hand-painted *Go Cougars!* sign
in school colors red and black.

Everyone's saying ...
Everyone's looking
at their phones ...

Everyone's saying

their mom

shot them

then killed herself.

Faces coming at me.
Voices smacking against me.
Ohmygod. Gracie. I can't believe it.
I just saw her.
So messed up.
Her little brother, how crazy is that?
Her mom! It was her mom!
How could she ohmygod.
I can't even, I've never
known anyone who—
So unreal ...

I am inside my body weaving
through the crowd.
Here
but not
here.

Sick rumor.
That's crazy.

It was a car crash
that killed all three.
It must have been.

There's no way.

Through the doorway
to my desk (third row, fifth seat).
I sit in Second Hour trigonometry.

Wait
for the
bell
to ring
because

I
don't
know
what
else
to do.

I Wish I Had a Sore Throat

I won't look at my phone.
At some point
the intercom crackles,
Daniel Valdez, please come to the office.

Mom has come to get me.
Standing outside the principal's office.
"*Mijo*," she calls me,
her voice breaking.

We hug and I sink into her.
My head on her shoulder.
My knees bent.
(I'm taller than her now.)

"How did you know?"

"They sent us an email.
Oh, Daniel! It's—unbelievable."

"Mom, everyone's saying
that Mindy—
it was a car crash, right?"

Mom stares at me,
confused.
Then her face crumples.

Choking on sobs, she tells me.

"Daniel,
Mindy shot them.
Then she killed herself."

"NO!

NO!"

She holds me.
Rocks me.
Rubs my back.

Whispers,
"I've got you.
I've got you."

Clinging to her, I am
instantly nine years old and
going home early
with a sore throat.

I wish

I was nine years old.

I wish

I had a sore throat.

Ding Ding Ding

We stop at Benny's Burgers
to get food
I can't eat.

I look at Mom's yoga pants.
Her long dark hair loose,
not in its usual tidy bun.

She never goes out in public
like this.

My phone dings and dings and dings and dings
and dings.
Texts from Trevor and Lydia.
Riley, Lashonda, Zach.

I try to answer.
Try to carry on
five different conversations.
None of us knowing what to say.
I suddenly hate
every
single
crying
emoji.

Later at home
I get calls from my sister Marissa
away at college.
And from Dad and Carrie.

Tommy, my stepdad, comes home early.
A back-slapping, hand-shaking guy,
he grabs me, holds me, won't let go.

Alone in my room,
I turn my phone to silent.
Close the blinds.
Stretch across my bed.
Sleep for three straight hours.

When I wake up—
throat dry
T-shirt damp with sweat—
for half a millisecond,

none of this

has happened.

I Know the Sidewalk

in front of Gracie's house.
Every crack, every bump.
Know the way it sounds
and feels
under my wheels.

Now the sidewalk is buried
under a sea of flowers and balloons
and more flowers.
Stuffed animals,
handmade cards, notes.
Flowers and votive candles
and more flowers.

A small crowd
of eight or ten people
stands quietly in the too-bright sunlight.
Why are kids here?

And then I realize they are
Abe's friends.
Seventh graders.
Twelve-year-olds.

I stare at the house remembering
all the times this summer.
Video game marathons.
Dinners of lasagna
or stir-fry chicken.
Hanging out by their pool after dark.

Now Gracie's empty house stares at me
through blank window eyes.

Yellow police tape surrounds the house.
Surrounds the
crime scene.

I walk away and leave

nothing.

Angels and Vultures

I was expecting
the grief counselors.

They arrived yesterday.
Swooping down on our high school like
angels.

Or vultures.

I was not expecting
the reporters.
Vans with satellite dishes,
giant antennas
pointing at the sky.

I was not expecting
cops holding back
the line of reporters.

It looks like every disaster scene
on the news I've ever seen.

"Excuse me—with the red backpack?
Did you know Gracie?
Can you say a few words?"

Some people walk over.
Microphones spring up.
The flock of vultures
shout questions.

Jasmine Alvarado, Olivia Thompson, Logan Dunn
look solemn while they answer.
Gracie didn't hang out with any of them.

I march over.
Grab a microphone.
"You weren't really
friends with her.
Do you even know
one single thing
about her?"

I throw down the microphone.
Crunch it under my foot.
Walk away.

But not really.

Instead, I clench my teeth.
Clutch the strap of my backpack
in a death grip.

Walk past the vultures and posers.

And then it hits me.
A gut punch.
At Hayden Junior High,
Abe's school,

I bet there are
flocks of vultures
there too.

When Your Friend Is Murdered

When your friend is murdered,
teachers are nice to you.

In our classes, we are given
new freedoms I want to give back:
Talking with friends.
Being on our phones.
Having unrestricted access
to the counselors.

During Third Hour, Trevor and I
huddle together.
He scrolls through his phone
showing me all the news stories.

He hasn't shaved for
a couple of days.
Weird how much older
the stubble on his chin
makes him look.

He imitates a reporter's voice:

"In the sunny desert of Glendale, Arizona,
with tidy suburban homes
surrounded by saguaro cactuses
and glistening backyard pools,
a community reels with grief over
the shocking deaths of ..."

I hold my hand up to
stop the oncoming traffic
of some journalist's take
on our lives.

Trevor stops reading.
Stares at his feet,
shakes his head.

I watch my knees bounce
with every jiggle
from my vibrating feet.

The ground under them
no longer feels stable.

Trevor says he's here for me
if/when I want to talk.

I nod and
say nothing.

"Maybe the grief counselors?"
he asks. Just to try it.

I say okay just to
get out of this room.
To make this endless day
go faster.

Stop Talking

We pick a small group
meeting in the library.

I know four of the seven people
sitting in the circle.
The fortyish woman talks soothingly
to some sophomore girl crying her eyes out.
Asks her to share a memory
of Gracie.

"Oh, I didn't—I never actually met her,"
the girl admits.

Michelle Griffin, a senior on the student council,
offers up words of wisdom,
that
EVERYTHING HAPPENS FOR A REASON

"… maybe a reason we small humans can't
understand but it's still important to …"

I'm not a
violent person.

But—
how great it would be to
shove my fist in her
stupid mouth to make her
stop talking.

I walk out the door

with the counselor
talking to
my back.

Chocolate Chip Pancakes

Mom tries to get me to eat something
by making my favorite breakfast
for dinner.

I realize
I am kind of starving.
And the pancakes are
soaked in butter and
smothered with
powdered sugar.

I eat two before I break into a cold sweat.
Run for the bathroom,
puking and coughing.
My stomach revolting against
me.

Mom is waiting with a cold
washcloth.
"*Mijo*, it's okay, I'll
get you some water."

"Mom! *Mom.* Listen—the police?
They got it wrong!
It was an *accident!*
Mindy would NEVER
have done that!

Maybe she was
showing them the gun,
warning them to never
touch it.

And somehow,
it must have gone off.
Maybe the bullet hit Abe and
Gracie was standing behind him.

And Mindy, she couldn't
live with herself so she
just lost it and that's how

it *really* happened."

Mom is crying now,
pulling me to her.
"Oh, Daniel, I wish, I wish
that's what happened.

But Mindy's friend Kathy said
she knew something was wrong.
Mindy was very depressed.
Isolating, not answering
texts or phone calls,
missing work."

Mom sobs, grips me tight.
Her wet tears soak my shirt.
"Daniel, I'd rather you
hear this from me."

Then she tells me.

Tells me Mindy planned it.

Tells me she left notes about the funerals.
Left important papers laid out carefully
on the kitchen table.
(I see the table where we
ate all those summer dinners ...)

Tells me Gracie and Abe were
sleeping in their beds when she
shot them.
(I see their rooms.
Smell the faint linseed oil ...)

Tells me Mindy called 911
saying she heard gunshots.
Then hung up and shot herself.
Left the doors unlocked so the police
would find them.
(I see the cops walking through
the same front door
I always walked through ...)

Now I am crying
gasping for breath
clutching my mother
begging her
please please promise me.
Promise me.

"Yes, *mijo!* Anything."

Poor Tommy stands by,
large and helpless.
Lets us cry all over each other.

"Mom, promise—
Promise you'll never kill me?"

She gasps out loud.
Nods, kisses me.

"I promise."

A Celebration of Life

Gracie's life should be celebrated, but

I want to skip this thing, this
memorial service at the high school.
It's pointless. It won't
bring her back.

Mom says "grieving rituals" help.
Tommy says we need to hold ceremonies—
weddings, baptisms, funerals—
to mark major life events.

I hug and get hugged by 20 or 30 people.
My friends and I sit in the auditorium,
everyone looking unnatural
in ties and jackets, dresses, drowning
in a sea of black.

The chorus sings.
The principal speaks.
Mrs. Kapoor, the art teacher,
shows slides of Gracie's art.
Tears flow.
Kleenex boxes get passed
down the rows.

Lashonda leans on me.
Rests her head on my shoulder.
I fold the paper program in half,
in quarters, in eighths. Drop it on the floor.
Kick it under my seat with my dress shoe.
Lashonda whispers I should keep it,
a memento, to remember.

To remember?
Like I could somehow forget?

Survived By

Gracie's dad is the last one
to speak, in town from
Colorado. He talks about
Gracie, thanks everyone
for coming. Tomorrow he'll go
to Abe's school, do the same thing
all over again.

That's it. It's over. No funeral.
Gracie and Abe are ashes now.
Their dad will take the two small
containers and spread them somewhere.

We line up to speak with the family.
I introduce myself to Gracie's dad.
His eyes light up. "So *you're* Daniel!"
Says he's heard all about me.
"Not just from Gracie—Abe, too."

We stand there shaking hands while I try
to speak, to say something.
But my throat closes up, my eyes are
swimming, blurry
until finally someone,
Zach maybe,

leads me away.

I hate grieving rituals.

My Father, Helpless

My dad wants to see me
even though it's a weeknight.
Even though I only go to
his and Carrie's on weekends.

"I just want to spend time
with you, that's all."

So he picks me up, just him.
Carrie's not with him which is
weird but he says she's
having a really hard time with this.

"Why?" I ask. "She never even
met Gracie. I don't think. Did she?"
Dad clutches the steering wheel,
stares at the car ahead of us, shrugs.

We go to Morgan's. Sit on the patio
overlooking the fake lake
where ducks float by living
their happy duck lives.

Josh, who'll be serving us this evening,
takes our drink orders.
Hands us menus.
Leaves us alone.

Dad asks how I'm doing.
When I say, "Okay," he says,
"No. I mean it. How *are* you?"

"Dad, what do you want me to say?"

He grips my shoulder,
stares intently at me.

We look alike.
Same compact build.
(We both wish we
were taller.)

Same dark hair,
thick and wavy.
But his getting gray
at his temples.

He opens his mouth and ...

nothing comes out.

My dad
    jogs five miles a day.
    Refurbishes old laptops to donate.
    Puts new brake pads on his Camry.
    Pays my orthodontist bills.
    Manages 10 people in his department.

And I realize
he doesn't know how

to fix this.

Some People

When we walk in the door
after dinner, Carrie hugs me tight.
She's crying now—she's been crying.
Her fair complexion
red and blotchy,
her blue eyes swollen.

She rubs my back in little circles
while I pat her back.
She's whispering to me
how awful it is, how sorry she is.

I got so mad at that sophomore girl.
The one who didn't even know Gracie.
Got so mad at those posers talking
to the reporters.

But seeing Carrie like this,
it's different. It shocks me
how upset she is,
how much she's crying.

Her blonde hair
hangs limp, unwashed.
Nails bitten and ragged.
She's maybe had a little too much
wine (she likes her wine). She's a little
unsteady, but Carrie's great,
my second mom.

She pulls away finally.
Wipes her runny nose
with a Kleenex.
Looks at me.

"Sweet boy," she says,
"Some people ..."
The tears are flowing again.

"Maybe some people don't deserve children."

Marissa

My sister surprises us all, walking in
Friday afternoon—home from college.
Unannounced, unexpected, greeted
with hugs and kisses.

Marissa is small for a big sister.
Ditched her contacts last year
in high school. Her thick
black-framed glasses suit her.
She looks right at me, standing on tiptoes,
putting her arms around me.

"How you doing?" "I'm okay."
Words that mean nothing, say nothing.
But our eyes carry on the deep conversation
our mouths would never speak.

Mom texts Dad the good news about Marissa.
He texts back *GREAT!* Says he'll see us
tomorrow. Marissa snacks on a kiwi,
yogurt, one graham cracker. Drinks a
bottle of sparkling water with lime.
Mom and Tommy quiz her
on classes, tests, papers. She loves her
zoology class, pre-calc grade is iffy.

Looks right at me. "How about a hike?"
Mom reminds us about dinner as we
grab water bottles and sunscreen.
Marissa reminds her about microwaves.
How they reheat leftovers magically.

Hike

We escape in her Civic. Just us.
The radio blasting. AC blowing cold air till
I switch it off, roll the windows down.
Let the warm air blow my hair back.

Riding toward South Mountain, city giving way
to desert. We park at a trailhead,
start climbing
up the trail. Feel the warmth radiating
from the rocks.
Dodging spindly ocotillo branches,
their thorns
reaching for the cotton cloth of T-shirts
or the skin of bare elbows.

Marissa reminds me of the time hiking
with Dad
when we rounded a turn on the trail,
almost stepped on a Gila monster—
how huge it was,
black and orange, sunning itself.
We keep climbing
past cholla cactuses and green-trunked
palo verde.

"It's awful, Daniel," Marissa says.
"The worst thing I've ever heard."
I take a swig of water, wipe my mouth. "Yep."
"If you wanna talk ..."
"Nope. Not really."
"Okay, I get that."

I scramble up a pile of rocks.
Take in the view.
Marissa, trying to join me, slips—
starts to fall.
I grab her. We clutch each other, chuckling.

A bird floats past us
across the bluest sky.
I want that bird's life.
Want to inhabit
its very being.

The Valley stretches out below us
miniature, neat, orderly. Streets on a grid,
Monopoly houses, dew-drop swimming pools.
Who could guess from here
the messes of the lives down there?

Maybe These Will Help

Later, in my room, a soft
tap-tap. Marissa's knock.
She slips inside, closes the door,
looks at me with a knowing smile.

"Hey, got something for you."
Hands me a round metal tin:
Cannabis-Infused Gummies.

"Oh, wow—seriously?"
I grin back at her. "Thanks!"

"Maybe these will help. If you can't sleep.
Just take half of one, okay?"
She's serious. Then she smirks.
Her voice drops to a playful whisper.
"And just don't, like, abuse them."
That makes us laugh.

"You mean, don't use them
as a gateway?" I whisper back.
"Don't buy an old RV
and start cooking meth?"

Marissa doubles over laughing.
"Exactly! Even though it's ..."
(she can't get the words out)
"... apparently quite lucrative!"
We're both laughing so hard.

Now maybe I can fly
like that bird in the sky.

Monster

That's what Mindy was.
According to
everybody.

You hear people talking about her
everywhere.
At coffee shops,
in line at the grocery store,
all over school.

Insane sick psycho. Why didn't she
just kill herself? How could a mom
do that? What was wrong
with her? She must have been
crazy or evil, pure evil.

It's easy to hate her.
But it's not that easy to explain her.

At least for me.

Why Did She Even

have a gun
in the first place?
Had she bought it to keep away
intruders, to scare away
bad guys?
Had she bought it to protect
her family? To keep them
safe?

Or did she buy it recently?
For what she was planning?

All those gun lovers say:
Guns don't kill people!
PEOPLE kill people!

Dude.
So don't let people have guns.

My Friends Are Sick

The way they won't stop
picking at the bloody scab
of what happened so it'll never
heal.

At lunch on Tuesday:

Trevor wonders:
"What's going to happen
to the house? Will they sell it or—"

Riley says:
"No one's ever going to
want to live there."

Lydia says:
"They should just
tear it down. I wish
the ground would open
and swallow it up."

Lashonda says:
"I went by there yesterday.
To look at the memorial.
Someone left a little Santa."

Zach says:
"What did they do with all
their stuff? Their clothes
and the furniture and everything?"

I shove
my tray back.
French fries go flying as
I storm out the door.

If

If I could predict
foresee
guess
sense.

If I could see their future
tell their fortunes
read their palms
chart their stars.

If I could turn back time and stop it.
Smell the danger and avoid it.
Feel the threat and escape it.
Find the gun and destroy it.

Then none of this would have
happened.

Turn Back Time

Turn back the clock.
Turn back the hours, the minutes.
Turn back back back to—

that Friday afternoon.
Gracie alive, unmurdered.
Abe alive, unmurdered.

Turn back time and redo
what happened.
Undo
what happened.

Do this instead:

When
Gracie asks if I want to hang out,
I say,
Sure, but let's go to my house instead.

And then Abe asks
if he can come, too.
And I say, *Sure.*

But wait—

That's not right. Abe is
shy. He'd never ask. So then

this happens:

I see Abe.
See his face. See his
I want to come, too look.

So I say *Hey, Abe, come with us!*
so we leave leave leave
the three of us together.
And go to my house where
Gracie and Abe are

safe, alive.

And then …

… then what happens?

Because when they do go home,
she's there.

Waiting.

So this happens:

Mindy kills
herself.
Herself only.
Just her.

And Gracie is safe, alive.
Abe is safe, alive.

And yes their beating hearts will break.
But at least they will be

beating.

I Never Saw

I never saw the monster.
Never saw her yell.
Never saw her angry.

I did see (what I thought was)
          a typical mom.
          Kind of quiet, like Abe.
          Polite to me.

She gave us space.
Let us hang out and laugh,
          play video games,
          raid the fridge.

She was a mom who
made her kids wear helmets.
Eat healthy snacks.
Come in at a reasonable hour.
Tell her where they were going and
who they would be with.

(I thought) she was a good mom.

Until she wasn't.

Signs

Did I miss them?
Fail to see them?

But if I missed them—
So did Gracie.
So did Abe.

At least I hope and pray they
never saw it coming.

Where's Your Rosary?

Mom asks one day
randomly.
"Where's your rosary?"

I shrug one shoulder,
shake my head.
"Don't know."

Don't *care* but
I don't say
that part out loud.

The rosary I got
for my First Communion.
When I was seven.

Not something
I keep handy for praying
whenever.

"It might help, Daniel.
It helps me. I say prayers
every morning.

I pray for all of them.
I pray for Gracie and Abe
and I pray for …"
Her voice cracks.
"I pray for Mindy, too."

I get off the couch,
walk over to hug her.
"Good, Mom. I'm glad it helps you."

What I don't say is
that it won't help
me.

Thank God

there's that mind-numbing THC.
Makes me buzzy and high as I please.
Eat a gummy each day,
I'll have no need to pray
'cause for a while my pain will cease.

Five Mothers, Minus One

My mom

prays, "Hail Mary."
Prays to a mom whose son
was killed. Prays for a mom who killed
her kids.

Mary,
full of grace, you
are blessed among women.
Please pray for us at the hour of
our deaths.

Mindy,
you loved your children.
Hugged them, kissed them, bathed them.
Gave them life and raised them. Then you
killed them.

Carrie,
no children call
you mama. Yet you can
still mother me and nurture me
always.

Gracie,
did you ever
dream of future, far-off
babies? Can you now see their sweet
faces?

Thanksgiving

The noise from all the relatives
like flocks of cawing birds. The mingling scents of turkey,
sage, tart cranberries, Aunt Alma's cigarettes. (Hasn't quit—
still trying.) My little cousin Mia cr-cr-crying.
Toni pulled out her hair ribbon. My 80-year-old *abuela*
asking something about school in Spanish. Laughing at me
saying *habla despacio*. The blessing Uncle Jaime says.
Yes to turkey. Mashed potatoes. Stuffing.
Not that green bean stuff.

Oh heck yeah, crescent rolls! A glass of wine maybe?
Mom says don't even. Oh, c'mon please? Okay, just a
sip. TV plays the same game all day, only the jersey colors
changing. Tommy and Uncle Gerry swearing,
pass, ah, they're gonna run it! Apple or pumpkin?
Why do you even ask, it's always apple. Yeah of course
ice cream.

Just don't ask me
what
I'm thankful for.

The First Time I Saw Gracie

Oh, I had seen her, but
not *seen* her,
since Mrs. Crawford's
kindergarten class.
Just one more girl out of
the corner of my eye.
Sitting on her sit-upon,
wheels on the bus go
round-and-round.

Round-and-round the playground
we ran: me, Matt, Isaiah, and Trevor.
Past the blur of faceless girls.
She might have been one of them if
I'd ever stopped to look. But why
bother? Nothing to see there.

Then third grade, Ms. Rosen?
Or maybe fourth grade, Mr. Pollack?
Gracie drew a picture that caught
my eye. A family flying kites high
in the sky. The colors popping
orange, red, yellow. I stared
at that picture. So much better
than every other. But didn't bother
to look
at
the artist.

In junior high, she must have
been there somewhere,
but I had eyes for Anna Nguyen.
Just eyes. I lost my voice, my nerve
whenever Anna came near. Never
stood a chance at that eighth grade
dance. Which makes me wonder—
where was she then?
I never looked to
see her.

Then freshman year—the skate park.
Me—seshing the quarterpipe when
this girl catches my eye.
Decent. Showing some steez.
But getting snaked
by these guys.
(Not enough that guys to girls is three to one,
you gotta snake 'em, too? Not cool.)

I watch her
five-oh a ledge,
land it clean.
Watch her take off
her helmet, shake
out her honey-colored hair.
She sees me seeing her and
smiles.

And that
was the first time
I saw
Gracie.

Abe and the World

There was that time when Gracie and I
helped Abe study for the geography bee.

Oh yeah, we helped him.
Tried to stump him.
Tossing around that inflatable
globe.

Spain, Bahrain, and Ukraine!
Uruguay, Paraguay, Norway, Zimbabwe!
Ghana, Grenada, Guatemala, and Guyana!
Kazakhstan, Afghanistan, Turkmenistan, Uzbekistan!
Latvia, Liberia, Liechtenstein, and Laos!

Shouting out countries and laughing.
Abe smiling, locating, pointing.

Here was a kid with the whole world
in his head.

The spinning orb of Earth
at his fingertips.

I didn't know until I read his
obituary, his real name was
Abel.

Hamster Life

That's what I'm living now.
Hamster life.
Running on the wheel.
Alarm shower coffee no breakfast
class class class lunch
class class class home.
Video games, a little homework if
I feel like it, but if
I don't the teachers are
oh so understanding. So
more video games dinner bed
sleep sometimes, sometimes not.
Now I take a gummy before school
instead of before bedtime.
They just make everything
fade away on this

hamster wheel.

School Home Repeat School Home Repeat School Home Repeat School Home Repeat School Home Repeat School Home Repeat School Home Repeat School Home Repeat

Virtual Life

A virtual life is the
best life.
In video games,
you decide how you look.
Face
hair
skin color
clothes.
You choose your world.
Dystopia
alien planet
football stadium
battlefield.
You can run
jump
swim
bounce off walls
fly.

Sure, you die a lot.
But you respawn
and have more lives.
Your health gets low,
down to one bar.
So you increase it
by finding objects.

You're working
toward a goal.
Fighting Nazis
scoring touchdowns
killing zombies
designing an alien city.

You always win.
If you don't win,
keep playing till you do.

One last thing:
You get to be a hero.

Weekends

On weekends, Dad and I
take hikes in the desert
now that the weather is nice.

Later, Carrie and I
play video games
(something I got her into).
And watch old movies
(something she got me into).

Carrie wants a ring
and a baby.
Dad wants to
keep things the same.

"I have a sneaky idea,"
she tells me as we
chase zombies through
a deserted town.

"For the Christmas party,
I'm going to tell everyone
to bring baby gifts as a gag.
Great idea, huh?

Little things like
a pacifier, a rattle, a bottle."
She giggles, sips her wine
(her two glasses turning into three).

Dad and Carrie always
have all the family over
for *la tamalada* where
we make hundreds of tamales.

I tell her I think it's
a funny idea, but
I doubt it'll work.
She can hope anyway.

When it comes to having kids,
Carrie sees a baby in a crib.
Dad sees teenagers with
problems he never imagined.

Not a Party

Zach texts, says come over.
We're gonna hang.
I say, *Who's we?*
He says everybody.
I say I'm not in the mood
for a party.
He says it's not a party,
just hanging out.

I arm myself first
with a gummy.
(Supply's getting low,
will let Marissa know
it's all I want for Christmas.)

I show up at Zach's and
everybody is there and
his parents are somewhere.
Music is playing and
1 gummy + 2 beers = cross faded faded faded
(I think I'm going to be sick).

Lashonda sits down on
the couch beside me.
She's a bit more fermented
than me (just a bit).
Lashonda's cute and curvy.
Sweet smile with dimples.
Dark hair, skin, eyes.

She messes up my hair, asks
why I'm always so angry.
"I'm not always so angry."
Lydia, Riley, and Lashonda all say,
"Oh yes, you are!"

Lashonda starts kissing
my nose. Eventually she
kisses my mouth and
I let her. Eventually I
kiss her back and
she lets me.

We're just friends, there's
nothing between us.
Now there's not even
space between us.
But this is
no big deal,
right?

Nighttime

These days I never know
if I'll sleep four hours or fourteen.
But I don't sweat it, I just
go with the flow.

These days, or I should say nights,
I never know if I'll dream or
wake dreamless or be sleepless.
But it's cool, it's alright.

Because nighttime is the right time
to wander silent streets alone.
My Vans pad softly, cat-like, and
everything surrounding me is mine.

Alone in these shadowy streets,
I glide past sleeping houses
full of sleeping people. Lulled
by my footsteps' steady beat.

I always walk now, never skate.
My board forgotten, dusty
in the corner while I roam.
Dreaming darkness slowly fades.

Flying

It starts off with Gracie and me skating
down my street in the brightest sunlight.
We're both pushing along going so fast
I can feel the wind blowing past me,
and Gracie's hair is streaming behind her.

And the tricks we're landing are blowing
our minds, every one first try.
Tre flips, 360 shuvs, varial flips.
We're wall riding up the side of every house
above the rooflines and dropping into
empty pools in every backyard.

And laughing—we can't stop laughing!
Because we're sending it and
our tricks are the sickest. And
then we see up ahead a huge crack
in the ground like an earthquake
opened up and Gracie yells,
"Watch me skate this gap!"

And she ollies across it. And
I'm watching so amazed
as she looks over her shoulder
and says, "See ya, Dez!"
and she keeps going.
Flying and flying—

And I wake up still feeling the rush,
and I'm
so happy.
Until I remember her flying away
from me.

Random

I've had something like
three, maybe four, dreams
about earthquakes.

That seems random.

Ghost

Lashonda says
I'm ghosting her.
Even though
I talk to her
practically every day.
And answer
most of her texts
eventually.

I say
I don't know
what she's talking about.
And she says
she senses something
between us.

I don't know
how to answer that
so I don't.

She texts that
she wants to know
what our "status" is.
And I make a
loud growling sound
I'm glad she
can't hear.

I don't answer
that text
either.

Gracie

Gracie—Grace.
Full of grace.
Fearless skater never backing down
from all the bros at the skate park.

Artist with bold crazy strokes
you could feel as much as see.
Color kaleidoscopes pulling you in,
making you part of the canvas.

Sharp sense of humor, easy to talk to.
Always herself, never playing games.
Determined, already taking on
the world.

Cute, natural, laid-back.
Tank tops and leggings.

Casual. Always
looked great even
with messy hair
or no makeup.

A good friend.
My best girl friend slash
friend who is a girl.
Potential girlfriend?

Maybe.
It did cross my mind, but
I didn't want to lose
what we had—

Our friendship
as comfortable as
a favorite cotton T-shirt.
Slip into it and be myself.

I didn't want to rush things,
and why should I? I thought
we had all

the time

in the world.

Bad Dream

I wake up yelling.
Turn the light on
breathing hard,
sheets wet with sweat.

It was just a dream.
It was just a dream.
You're awake now.
It wasn't real.

Light

Turn on all the lights.
Keep your feet on the bed
just in case.
The closet door is
cracked partway.
Hum the Mister Rogers theme song.
How long till
daylight?

Coffee

It's still dark at 5:30,
but
all the lights are
on in the kitchen.
And the
smell of coffee
seems very
normal.
And
everything is okay
I think.

I drink
the coffee and
look in all
the corners but
not out the window, but
everything is okay
I think.

Mom gets up at 7:00 and
smiles at me, saying,
"You're up early!"
I look at her.
I think
she looks normal, and
everything is okay
I think.

So I say, "Yeah.
I woke up early."
I look at her.
I look at the
knife drawer,
but
everything is okay
I think.

It's Not a Dream

when you are a zombie
and everyone you love
is killing you over and over.
Your mom kills you
with a sickle.
And
your stepmom kills you
with a hammer.
And
your dead friend kills you
with a knife.
But it's really hard to
kill a zombie and
you don't die easily.
Still they keep killing you
over and over.

And when you're yelling
but the only thing that comes out
are those throaty zombie noises.
And you WANT to die
because they hate you and
they want you dead.
And when you wake up
it's not a dream.

It's a nightmare.

That will haunt you.

Even when you're

awake.

Crash and Burn

The second I see the trig test,
I know I'm going to fail it,
but it's okay really.

I sit there for 50 minutes
listening to pencils scratching on paper
and the soft *tick tick* of the clock.

I think about how
two months ago
this would have
mattered and how now
it doesn't.

But It Does Matter

to my parents when they find out
that not only did I fail the trig test,
but I didn't even bother to answer
one single question.
And then they find out that
I'm failing all my other classes
except for driver's ed.

And so we must go in for a
conference, and I'm wondering
which of my many parents
to take. And I ask if it can be
Dad because I'm mostly over
the zombie dream
but not quite.

HELP

It is decided
that I need
HELP.
Professional Help
after all
the shock
trauma
grief
I've been through.

So
phone calls are made
and
appointments are set.

I'm Really Okay

I try to convince them that
I can bring my grades up.
Promise I'll catch up on
all the missed homework.
Swear that I don't need
Professional Help.
Assure them all that
I'm really okay.

Mom tells me
my appointment is at
4:00 on Tuesday.

I hope that
I don't
have to
talk about
my dreams.

Kyle Liu, MS, LPC

Kyle (he tells me to call him that)
asks me to take a seat, which
feels like a test because
there are two chairs and a
short couch and a
bigger couch.

"Where?" I ask.

"Anywhere," he says.

I pick the short couch.

He picks a chair.

Kyle is young—30s, I guess?
In jeans, a T-shirt, flip-flops.

He looks like some random guy
who wandered into this office.
I'm a therapist, really,
I swear.

He doesn't say anything and
I wonder if I'm supposed to
start.

Finally after a long pause, he
asks me why I'm here.

"Because my parents are making me."

<Pause>

"And why is that?"

"Because I'm failing all my classes."

<Pause>

(This guy is really rocking
a chill Zen vibe.)

I have a feeling that
counseling with Kyle
is going to be full of

long pauses.

Counseling with Kyle

Eventually the real reason
I'm here comes up.

He asks me about it.

I tell him he can
read the gory details online
if he wants them.

He says we don't have to talk
about it, we can talk about
whatever I want to.

That sounds fine, but the things
I'd normally want to talk about
(gaming, skateboarding)
are kind of off-limits, too.

He asks if I want to play some
air hockey.

Uh—YEAH, I think.
"Okay," I say.

Mean Moves

He says we'll play a match,
best two out of three.
But after I beat him the first two,
I ask if we can still play the third
anyway.

He says sure. He says
I have some mean moves.
I guess because of the way
I slam the puck.

"Anger is a common emotion
that comes with grief.
People who haven't experienced
grief firsthand think it's just
about being sad.
But anger, even rage, is
quite common."

The puck glides across the air holes.
Our red paddles *clack clack*.
Kyle plays defense, guarding his goal.
But I play out front offensively,
my paddle up near the center line.

"People experience a wide range
of emotions. Confusion. Guilt.
Abandonment. Even envy.
Some people envy their loved ones
because they feel like they're
in a better place."

I let him score on me once, twice,
otherwise the game would be over.

"The main thing is to deal with
emotions in a constructive way."

"Like kicking your butt in air hockey?"
I say.

I shoot the puck hard to the right edge
so it banks and drops smoothly
into the slot of his goal.

"Like kicking my butt in air hockey,"
Kyle says.

Fine

Mom wants to know
how it went.
"Fine," I say.
I tell her that
Kyle says
we'll do
four sessions.
Maybe
schedule
more
"if needed."

I do not
tell her
we spent most
of the session
playing
air hockey.
I want her
to think
she's getting
her money's worth.

"I think it'll help," I say.

"I hope so, *mijo*," she says.

Was

For this session, Kyle suggests
something different. On a table
there are piles of cut-out pictures
from magazines, a few small squares
of poster board, and a glue stick.

"How about an art collage today?"

"No air hockey?"

"Let's do this first."

I sit down, letting my hands shuffle
through all the pictures
and also cut-out words.
At first not seeing much I like.

Pulling some out and
setting them aside and
a few more.
Taking the top off the glue stick.
Thinking how I haven't held
one of these since maybe fourth grade,
and this is nice and distracting.

An eyeball.
The word DON'T.
Wrecked powder blue Mustang.
Tree stump.
Dried-up cracked ground.

"Gracie was an artist. She was
really good. She painted. Mostly
abstract with really bright colors."

Kyle inserts one of his Zen pauses.

I glue down my pictures
shuffle through the stack
pull out some more.

"I hate that word, by the way."

<Zen pause>

Finally,
"What word is that?"

"Was."

<Zen pause>

"I hate the word *was*.
I hate thinking of her
in past tense."

Kyle nods,
says

<nothing>

Giant Stuffed Panda

Randomly I insert a
giant stuffed panda
in the lower corner of my collage.

The panda is the pause
in our sessions.
Quiet
immense
soft
comforting.

It's just me,
Kyle,
and
a
giant stuffed panda
in the room, and
I like it.

Heaven or Something

There is something I
think about a lot,
so I bring it up with Kyle.
It's this:

"I wonder where Gracie is?"

He waits for me to say more.

"I mean—I know she's dead and
I know she was cremated and
her ashes were scattered
somewhere."

He waits for me to say more.

"But I wonder where
SHE is.
That part of her
that was Gracie."

"Where do you think she is?" asks Kyle.

"I don't know. I mean, I know
what Catholics believe,
but I don't know
if that's what happens
when people die.

Maybe she's in
Heaven or something
like that. Or maybe
she'll be recycled into
a new life. Or maybe
there's nothing
left of her
at all."

"Where do you hope she is?" he asks.

"It doesn't matter where *I* hope she is.
I could hope she's in a field of
wildflowers or floating on white puffy clouds with wings
and a halo.
But if those places don't *exist*, then it doesn't matter
what I hope for her, does it?"

A Suggestion

"If Gracie were here right now,
what would you say to her?" asks Kyle.

"She's not here," I say. "So what does it matter?"

"This is just a suggestion," says Kyle.
"You could try talking to her.
You're right. She's not here.
And that's terrible. Terrible
to the nth degree."

"I don't know if she can hear you.
I don't know if she's around somewhere.
I don't know if she's in Heaven.
I don't know if she's simply gone.

None of us really knows, do we?
We have our beliefs but
we don't really know
for sure.
And that's hard.

But you could try
talking to her.
Or writing her a letter."

"It's just a suggestion," he offers.

"It's a stupid suggestion," I say.

"Well," says Kyle. "It's only a suggestion."

Dear Gracie

I hope you're okay.
I hope you and Abe are together.
I hope there's a Heaven.

You ~~were~~ are and always will be
an amazing person and a great friend.

I think about you every single day.
I miss you every single day.

Gracie—
everything I just wrote
sounds lame.
Whatever words
I think of aren't
big enough
to tell you
how I feel.

These words are
a rough patch
of asphalt.

But how
I feel about you
is
the whole
spinning
world.

And now the
world is broken
into pieces.

P.S.

I hope
it was over
before you even
knew
what happened.

Dez

Carrie and I are watching an old movie.
A comedy about a zany woman who
keeps calling a nerdy guy Steve
even though his name is Howard.

It's actually pretty funny,
which explains why
I start to cry and
I can't stop.

Carrie hugs me, rocks me, but
I can't stop.
All the tears I haven't cried
I'm crying now.

Finally I choke out words:
"Gracie always called me Dez.
No one's ever going to
call me Dez again."

Now Carrie is crying and
she can't stop.
I try to comfort her but
she can't stop.

"This whole community is hurting.
It's affected everyone," she says.
"It's affected me ... so much ..."
She shakes her head,
pours a little more wine.

Phone Call

"Dad?"

"Hey, sorry to call you at
school. You're at lunch
now, right?"

"What's wrong?"

"Carrie's in the hospital.
For observation."

"Why?"

"She's okay. But
last night she took some
sleeping pills, and
she'd been drinking."

"WHAT?! Did she—"

"She's awake now and she's
talking."

"Dad! Was it—did she
do it
on purpose?"

"Ahh. Well.
That's what we're trying
to figure out."

Heart Attack

I am seriously having a
heart attack.
Terrible pain in my stomach,
my knees drawn up, moaning.
My breathing all gaspy, shallow.
Sweating, shaking alone in my room.
Nobody else home.
Should call 911.
Call Kyle instead,
leave a voicemail.
He calls back 10 minutes later.
Says it's a panic attack.
Talks me through
breathing exercises

until the pain
slowly
fades.

One by One

It feels like
everyone I love
is going to be
ripped away from me
one by one.

When is it ever
going to stop?

Drowning

Before, I barely cried at all.
Now I can't stop.
I cry at night in bed softly.
I cry alone as I walk the dark streets.
I cry in the shower so no one hears me.

I cry pattering misty rains.
I cry raging monsoon rains.
I cry till I dry up and think
it's over until
I cry again.

I can't tell.
Is this a good thing?
Or a bad thing?

Something Bad

Carrie, out of the hospital, no longer being observed,
texts me, asks
if I want to get breakfast.
I'm on winter break now. I text back,
Yep, can't wait to see you.

I hug her across the front seat console.
Then we're silent, waiting for the other
to go first, the turn signal a loud heartbeat
between us.

We get some bagels and go to the park,
sit on the hard benches of a picnic table.

I ask
if she's okay.

She says
she is.

I ask
if she did it on purpose.

She says
she didn't.

I say
it'll seriously kill me
if I lose anyone else.

She says
I won't.
"Daniel, there's something
I want to tell you.

"Okay."

"Something bad.
Really bad."

"Okay."

Dark Secret

Then she tells me. About how
when she was 16, my age,
she got pregnant and got an abortion
using her older sister's ID.
"I think the receptionist knew,
but she didn't say anything.
We looked a lot alike."

She says she never told
anybody except her sister.
Not her parents, her brother,
any of her friends.
It's been this
dark secret
she's kept hidden
from everyone.

"Even your dad. I never told him."
I wonder why she's picked me
to tell this to now, but I don't ask.
I do ask if the father knew, and
she starts to cry.

She says that's the worst part.
She never knew who it was.
She'd been to a party
drank too much
couldn't remember.

"You know how I said
some people don't
deserve children?

I think I'm one of those people.
Maybe I don't
deserve them
either."

Quoting Kyle

I spend that night
at Dad and Carrie's,
the two of us staying
up late talking.

Carrie is
relieved to talk about her "dark secret"
ashamed of what happened
happy to punish herself forever.

I tell her
she was a scared kid.
It wasn't her fault.
There's nothing to be ashamed of.
It was rape if she blacked out.
She did what was best for her at the time.
She needs to forgive herself.
Counseling might help.

She reminds me I didn't
want to do counseling,
asks me if it's helped.

I say yes it has helped,
and I mean it.
I didn't think it was helping,
but it is.

"Carrie, you're being brave.
You're brave to let yourself
feel all this pain.
It takes strength to do
what you're doing."

I can't say anything
more because
the words choke me
into silence.

That's word for word
what Kyle
told me.

Christmas

I'm not in the spirit
this year. But somehow
all the traditions
pull me in and
I have moments,
even days,
when I feel
the cheer.

Decorations, the tree,
wrapping presents.
All the cooking and baking.
Holiday movies.
Luminarias along the driveway
on Christmas Eve.

We make tamales, but
Carrie doesn't go through
with the baby gag gifts.
I turn down the gummies
from Marissa, because I'm done
hiding from my problems.
I know I need to face them
with a clear head.

Now it's almost
the New Year.

A new beginning.

And a year with
no Gracie
in it
at all.

Hold Tight

I'll hold tight
to you this year
and the next
and every year
after that
forever.

Stay with me
in my heart
in my soul.

That's where
you live now.

P.S.

It actually
does help
to talk
to you.

Better

I spend the break
catching up on old assignments.
My teachers have been understanding,
but I need to do the work.
So I do.

Mom says one evening,
"You seem better.
I'm so happy to see that."

"Do I? Better how?"

"You're sleeping better.
You were either sleeping
too much or not enough.
And your appetite—it's coming back."

"Kyle says my body was grieving.
It was affecting me physically.
He said it's not just emotions."

Mom nods, gets tearful.
"Ever since you were a baby,
I've tried to protect you,
keep you safe.
But I can't keep the world
from hurting you."

"I'm never going to get over this."

"I know, *mijo*."

"I'm just trying to *feel* better.
Turn my wounds into scars."

"That's all you
can do, my son."

Scars

One on my forehead
near my hairline
about an inch long
from when I fell against the end table
in the living room when I was two.

On my knee, a raised lumpy one
from crashing my bike, probably
should've had stitches but didn't.

The road rash on my right elbow,
a bunch of little gravel indentations
from a skateboarding wipeout
(looks pretty sick actually).

And now a few more
on my soul.
I wonder what those
look like.

Ghost 2.0

I text Lashonda,
ask her if she wants to
get coffee with me.

She leaves me
unread.

Okay.
I get that.

Aftershocks

My sessions with Kyle
are winding down, only
a couple more to go.

We've talked about Mindy, about
why she did it. If maybe in
some twisted way she thought
"taking them with her"
was better than
leaving them behind.

I let out a sigh, lean my head back,
stare at the wall. I feel Kyle waiting
for me to say something else.

"It wasn't a ripple effect what she did.
It wasn't any stone in a pool of water.
It was—

it was an earthquake. It shook
everyone and ripped our world open.
And we—

we keep finding new signs of

damage,

and the ground under everyone's feet
doesn't feel safe anymore. And

it might never feel safe again.

I'm done talking about her, okay?"

"Okay."

Memorial

"So what do I do now?"
I ask.

"What would you like to do
to remember Gracie?"

"The school is planting a tree.
Abe's school is doing that, too."

"Okay, that's nice, but
I mean you personally.
Is a tree the best way
for *you* to remember her?"

"Not really. I mean, at least they're
doing something. A tree will live
for a really long time, but …"

"What kind of memorial would you like to have for Gracie?"

"I'm not sure."

"Maybe that's something to think about."

Grieving Rituals

"So these are grieving rituals
I guess?" I say.

"What's that?" asks Kyle.

"These are grieving rituals, right?
Having a funeral.
Planting trees.
Making a memorial.
Doing something
instead of trying not to
think about it."

"Right.
Grieving rituals are an active way
of acknowledging death."

"I guess I get that."

Do Not Erase Her

It feels like the horrible way
she died has taken over
who Gracie was.
Like her
violent shocking
death
erased her life.

Her life may have ended,
but it wasn't erased.
I won't let her death
erase her life.

Her life has to leave a mark.
It has to.

OK

I text Lashonda again. This time
an apology saying that I treated her
really bad and I'm sorry and
she's a really good friend and
I'm afraid of losing her.

She finally responds
OK.
And I ask again
if she wants to
get coffee. And she
leaves me unread again
for an hour, but

she finally responds
OK.

Coffee with a Friend

It goes better than I thought.
We meet and I'm straight
with her, saying if she's wanting
a relationship I can't right now.
I'm just trying to get through
every single day.

She asks if I was
in love with Gracie.
I start to get mad.
What was between
Gracie and me
has nothing to do with her.
I'm not going to answer.

But then I say
I definitely loved her,
and I'll never get over this.

"No, I know.
None of us will."

"I'm sorry if I hurt you.
It's just that I was hurting.
But that's no excuse."

"No, it's not."

"So. You forgive me?"

She flashes her
sweet, dimpled
smile.
Covers my hand
with hers.

"I'll try."

Amazing

Carrie texts me,
tells me
she's had two sessions
with her new counselor.

OMG! I can't believe how
amazing it is just to talk to
somebody.

I've kept this secret for
soooo long it's
a huge relief to
let it out.

That's awesome!

She's also
referring me to a doctor.
To prescribe antidepressants.

Are you OK with that?

Yep! More than OK!!
(thumbs-up emoji)

btw you're amazing

No, you are!
(kissing emoji)

What If ...

I'm kind of surprised that
Carrie's counselor thinks
she needs medication.

If Carrie needs it, then
Mindy definitely did.
She needed it more
than anybody.

What if she'd gotten it?
What if instead of
buying a gun
she went to a doctor?

Incredibly Beautiful

Today's my last session.
I'm wired, but
in a good way.

"You seem
excited?" Kyle says.

"I guess I am.
I think I've figured out
what I want to do
for Gracie's memorial."

I tell him

it's complicated.
I'm not exactly sure
how to get it done.
It'll involve
a lot of people.
It's not as easy as
planting a tree.

He asks if I
want to tell him
what it is.

So I do.

<Pause>

"It's what I want to do.
I think it's perfect.
I think she'd love it.
It's very Gracie,
you know?"

Kyle is quiet
as he listens to me.

Finally he says,
"It sounds
incredibly beautiful."

A smile I wasn't expecting
escapes me.

"Good.
Because that was Gracie.
Incredibly beautiful."

What It Is

What it is
is a mural
of Gracie's artwork
at the skatepark.

That's it.
That's what
I want to do.

Leave a Mark

I tell Mom and Tommy,
Dad and Carrie
my idea.
I text Marissa.
They tell me it's
great, perfect, very fitting.

At school I tell Lydia
first because she was
Gracie's best friend.
She cries, hugs me.

At lunch I tell
Trevor and Zach,
Lashonda and Riley.
They tell me I seem
excited, focused.

After school I talk to
the art teacher, Mrs. Kapoor.
She says it will be a
lovely tribute.

We look through
Gracie's artwork,
pick out possible pieces.
There are so many,
it'll be hard to decide.

But I'm excited,
even a little bit
happy.

And I can't wait
to do this.
Help Gracie leave
her mark
on the world.

Big News

Friday evening Dad and Carrie
pick me up and we head to
Bangkok Palace for dinner,
Carrie's favorite.

Dad and Carrie are showing
a lot of PDA,
and Carrie says,
"We have some big news."

I look at Carrie,
look at my dad,
both smiling.
"You're *pregnant?*"

They laugh, shake their heads.
"No!"
"Not yet!"
"But we are getting married."

"Oh," I say. "Nice.
Congratulations."
They're still laughing at me.
"You sound disappointed," Carrie says.

I shrug. Tell them
a wedding is cool but
not as cool as
a little brother. Or sister.

They say no promises,
but that could still happen
later.
Which is great.

"Anyway, it won't be
that different," I say.
"You've been together so long
it's like you're already married."

Dad nods, nudges Carrie.
"Exactly what I've always said."
Carrie shoves him playfully.
"So why not put it on paper?"

"My commitment to you
is so much stronger than
a piece of paper," Dad says
and kisses her.

We toast the happy couple.
I'm smiling and it feels so good
to feel good again.

Coming Together

On a warm morning
late in February,
we meet at
the skatepark:
    Mrs. Kapoor
    Gracie's dad
    two local artists
    a city councilwoman
    me.

It's a weekday.
(I got excused from
American history.)
The park's mostly empty.

We walk around.
I point out
different features:
the bowl
halfpipe
quarter pipe
jump ramp
manual pad.

The artists and
Mrs. Kapoor discuss
the logistics of where
to paint Gracie's art.

These artists, Sergio and Victor,
are legit with their own business
painting giant murals
all around the city.

Mrs. Kapoor found them,
told them about our project.
They'll reproduce Gracie's art,
donating their time and their talents,
which is huge, awesome.

My friends and I are raising money
at school to buy all the paint and supplies.
Ms. Martinez Reyes from the city council
is helping us get our proposal ready.

Lots of emails back and forth
with Gracie's dad, and now
he's here, a part of this.
Choosing his favorite paintings,
telling us stories.

Gracie as a preschooler
couldn't get enough of
crayons, markers, finger paints.
He's excited, grateful, emotional.

"She would love this," he says
over and over.
"She would love this."

I can't believe
how it's
coming together.

It'll take
months
lots of planning
a chunk of change
a team of people.

But it's coming together.
It's going to happen.
For Gracie.

Help Us Heal

A mom with a preschooler on a scooter
has been watching us. And now as
the rest of the group walks away
she stops me. Asks me if
this has something to do with
the two kids who were killed.

I say yes, tell her about Gracie's art.
Say that Gracie and Abe were my friends.
Point out their father in the group.

She says it's wonderful what we're doing.
"It'll help us heal."
She covers her face,
hides her tears, her red eyes.

She apologizes to me, says she
has no right to cry.

"Sure, you do.
It affected everybody.
Not just the people who
knew them."

She nods, tells me
she can't wait to see it.

"Thanks," I say.
"Me too."

Sunrise

It looks like a sunrise.
Swirls of pink clouds
across the deck.
The nose gold.
The tail orange.
Bright yellow
around the trucks.
Fuchsia wheels
rimmed black.

Gracie's board.
The deck she
painted herself.
The board
her dad gave me.
Said she'd want me
to have it.

The thing about
skateboarding is
if you do it enough
you're going to break
a lot of decks.
It happens.
You just get
a new one.
Mount your
trucks and wheels,
and you're good to go.

So I won't skate
with this board often.
But I will today
this morning
the first time
I've been on a board
since that Friday.

I drop the board,
the clatter of
polyurethane wheels
against asphalt.
Black Vans against
black grip tape.
Push off, ready to
pop the first trick.

Hit it, Dez!

"Okay," I say.
"Le's getit!"

Grief Resources for Teens

Are you dealing with grief from the death of a friend or family member? Help is out there. Check out some of these resources:

- Actively Moving Forward® is a national network to address the needs of grieving young adults. Their mission is to help teens "actively move forward" in memory of their lost loved one. Visit their website at https://healgrief.org/actively-moving-forward/

- You can also download the AMF App for additional tools and resources. If you register, you'll have access to virtual support groups, grief coaches, community boards, videos, and more: https://healgrief.org/amf-app/

- Dougy Center, located in Portland, Oregon, has a Teen Resources page. You can use filters to search by **Topic or Type of Death and Person Who Died** to find articles, podcasts, and activities to help you: https://www.dougy.org/resources/audience/teens

- The National Alliance for Children's Grief offers resources for teens and kids who are grieving. You can search for programs near you, including support groups, individual counseling, and school-based programs. A filter also lets you search for free services: https://nacg.org/find-support/

- Your school counselor—check with counselors at your school for grief support services in your local area.

WANT TO KEEP READING?

If you liked this book, check out another book from West 44 Books:

THE DRAGONS CLUB
BY CYN BERMUDEZ

ISBN: 9781978596047

VIOLIN

I play my violin:
wind-bow-resin-rain.

An extension of forefinger,
hand, and arm. Of me.

Gliding across tight stings.
A song, like the bellow of a horn,

pulled from my heart,
from the deep seat of my soul.

As if all that I feel would swallow me,
overwhelming me like a tidal wave.

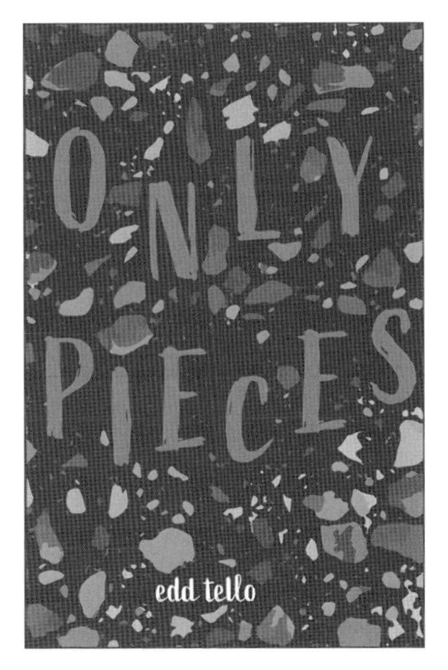
ONLY
PIECES
edd tello

THE
BEST
PART IS
AT THE
END

RIGHT
ON
CUE

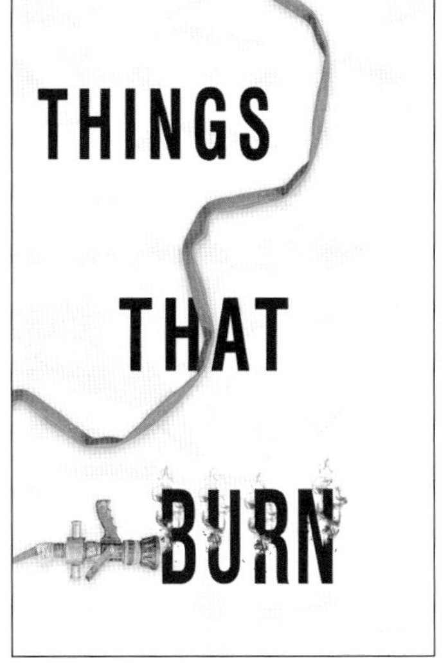
THINGS
THAT
BURN

About the Author

Katy Grant is the author of nine novels for young readers. For many years, she taught creative writing and composition courses at the college level. A native of Tennessee, she now lives in Arizona with her husband. She enjoys travel, hiking, biking, and spending time with her two adult sons.